This book belongs to :

Anna's Birthday Adventure

安娜生日探險記

Allan Frewin Jones 著

Judy Brown 繪

本局編輯部譯

三民書局

Chapter One

It was Anna's birthday. At last! She woke up feeling very, very excited. She ran down the stairs two at a time.

"Happy Birthday!" said Mum and Dad together.

"Hooray!" shouted Anna as she saw the pile of presents on the living-room floor. She had some really wonderful presents. She was still **ripping wrapping** paper and **tearing tissue** when Granny arrived on her **motorbike** and gave Anna yet another present.

第一章

　　安娜的生日終於到了！醒來後安娜興奮地三、兩步衝下樓去。

　　「生日快樂！」爸爸媽媽齊聲說。

　　「萬歲！」安娜一看見客廳地上成堆的禮物，就大叫了起來。有些禮物真的很棒。就在她忙著撕開包裝紙的時候，奶奶騎著摩托車來了；當然又送給她一份禮物。

rip [rɪp] 動 撕開
wrapping [`ræpɪŋ] 名 包裝紙
　wrapping paper 包裝紙
tear [tɛr] 動 撕裂
tissue [`tɪʃu] 名 薄紙
motorbike [`motɚ,baɪk] 名 摩托車

What a **brilliant** birthday!

Suddenly Anna realized something.

"Where is Uncle Oscar's present?" she asked. "Uncle Oscar **promised** to send me a very special present this year."

Anna had never met her Uncle Oscar. She

knew he lived on a **tiny** island off the north coast of **Scotland**. Uncle Oscar's island was called the **Isle** of Chyppes, and it was the last island before the big wide ocean. If you were in a ship and you didn't stop at the Isle of Chyppes, you wouldn't see dry land again for six whole weeks.

多棒的生日呀！

突然間安娜想起一件事。

「奧斯卡叔叔的禮物在哪兒呀？」她問。「奧斯卡叔叔答應今年要送我一份非常特別的禮物呢！」

安娜從來沒有見過奧斯卡叔叔，她只知道他住在蘇格蘭北海岸的一個小島上。奧斯卡叔叔的小島叫做凱普斯島，它是你駛入汪洋大海前所能看到的最後一座小島；也就是說，如果你的船不在凱普斯島靠岸的話，接下來的六個星期，你可能都看不到陸地了。

brilliant [`brɪljənt] 形 出色的，燦爛的
promise [`pramɪs] 動 承諾
tiny [`taɪnɪ] 形 極小的
Scotland [`skatlənd] 名 蘇格蘭
isle [aɪl] 名 小島

Uncle Oscar had spent years traveling all over the world, **exploring sweltering** jungles and climbing **gigantic** mountains and **diving** into great big rivers and being lowered on ropes into deep, dark caves. He was **enormously** rich and had **retired** to a tall stone tower on the Isle of Chyppes to write his life story.

奧斯卡叔叔常年在世界各地旅行，在悶熱的叢林裡探險、爬高山、潛入壯闊的大河，甚至還綁著繩索，下到又深又黑的洞穴內。他非常有錢，退休後他就在凱普斯島高聳的石頭碉堡上，寫他一生的故事。

explore [ɪk`splɔr] 動 探險
sweltering [`swɛltərɪŋ] 形 酷熱的
gigantic [dʒaɪ`gæntɪk] 形 巨大的
dive [daɪv] 動 潛水
enormously [ɪ`nɔrməslɪ] 副 非常地
retire [rɪ`taɪr] 動 退休

A few weeks ago Uncle Oscar had written a letter to Anna.
The letter said this:

Dear Anna

*I am very sorry that I have been too busy exploring to have ever met you. I would like to **make up for** this by buying you a very special birthday present on your next birthday. I am afraid I don't know what girls like for birthday presents. Please write to me with a **list** of the sort of presents you would like.*

Yours truly

Uncle Oscar

幾個星期以前，奧斯卡叔叔寫了一封信給安娜，內容是這樣的：

　　親愛的安娜

　　很抱歉我一直都忙著探險，結果連見妳一面的機會都沒有。今年我打算買樣非常特別的生日禮物送給妳做為補償，可是我不知道女孩子會喜歡哪些生日禮物，可不可以請妳列出一張清單，告訴我妳喜歡的生日禮物。

　　愛妳的

　　奧斯卡叔叔

make up for 補償

list [lɪst] 名 名單

Anna had written a letter to Uncle Oscar, thanking him for thinking of her (this was her mum's idea) and **enclosing** a list of things she would like for her birthday (these were all Anna's ideas).

And now the morning of her birthday had arrived. But a special birthday **parcel** from Uncle Oscar **definitely** hadn't arrived!

安娜便寫了一封信給奧斯卡叔叔，感謝他還惦記著她(這是媽媽的主意)，再附上一長串她想要的生日禮物(這些才是安娜的主意)。

　　現在已經是生日當天的早上了，可是奧斯卡叔叔那特別的生日禮物顯然還不見蹤影。

enclose [ɪn`kloz] 動 附上
parcel [`pɑrsl̩] 名 包裹
definitely [`dɛfənɪtlɪ] 副 顯然地

"Perhaps he forgot," said Anna's mum. "You must remember that your Uncle Oscar is a very **unusual** man. And unusual men sometimes forget things that **ordinary** people remember. I'm sure he didn't **mean** to **upset** you."

"I'm not upset," said Anna trying her best not to look upset.

「或許他忘記了，」安娜的媽媽說，「不要忘了，奧斯卡叔叔是位不平凡的人，不平凡的人有時會忘記平凡人所記得的事情。我相信他不是有意要讓妳難過的。」

　　「人家才沒有難過咧！」安娜盡量讓自己看起來一點都不難過。

unusual [ʌnˈjuʒʊəl] 形 不平凡的
ordinary [ˈɔrdn̩ˌɛrɪ] 形 平常的
mean [min] 動 有意
upset [ʌpˈsɛt] 動 使沮喪 形 難過的

Chapter Two

Mum and Dad had to go and do some shopping. Granny stayed with Anna and **showed** her how to make an armchair into a **perfect** tent by **tipping** it over on to its side and **hanging** a table cloth over it.

Anna and her granny sat in their tent and watched television through a small **gap** in the table cloth.

"It's much more fun watching television like this," Granny said. "I don't know why more people don't do it." Granny smiled at Anna. "Are you having a nice birthday?" she asked.

第二章

爸爸和媽媽必須外出買些東西，奶奶留在家裡陪伴安娜。奶奶教她把扶椅側躺，然後披上桌巾，做成一個完美的帳篷。

安娜和奶奶躲在帳篷裡面，透過桌巾的縫隙看電視。

「這樣看電視有趣多了，」奶奶說，「真搞不懂大家為什麼不這樣做。」然後奶奶笑著問安娜：「過生日快不快樂呀？」

show [ʃo] 動 教
perfect [`pɝfɪkt] 形 完美的，正確的
tip [tɪp] 動 將…翻倒《over》
hang [hæŋ] 動 掛
gap [gæp] 名 縫隙

Anna nodded. "Yes," she said. "It's very nice. But I still wish Uncle Oscar's present had arrived. Do you think he forgot all about me?"

"I don't know," said Granny. "But there's one way to find out."

"We could telephone him!" said Anna.

"He doesn't have a telephone," said Granny. "But if you asked me, I'd say that the best way of finding out what happened to your birthday present would be to go up to your Uncle Oscar's house, **knock** on the door and say 'Hello, Uncle Oscar, how do you do? I'm your **niece** Anna and it's my birthday today **in case** you *forgot.*' "

「嗯！」安娜點點頭說。「是很棒啦！不過我還是希望能收到奧斯卡叔叔的禮物。您想他是不是把我忘得一乾二淨了？」

「這我就不知道了，」奶奶回答說，「但是一定有辦法找到答案的。」

「我們可以打電話給他！」安娜說。

「他沒有裝電話。」奶奶說。「可是如果妳問我該怎麼辦，我想弄清楚你生日禮物下落最好的辦法就是到奧斯卡叔叔家中，敲敲大門說：『嗨！奧斯卡叔叔，您好嗎？我是您的姪女安娜，順便提醒您今天是我的生日。』

knock [nɑk] 動 敲
niece [nis] 名 姪女，外甥女
in case... 以防…，免得…

"But it's such a long way," sighed Anna. "How would I *ever* get there?"

"I could take you on my motorbike," said Granny.

"Wow!" said Anna, and the next thing she knew she was sitting behind her granny on the great big motorbike, **wearing** a **helmet** that nearly covered her eyes while they **zoomed** along the road at a great speed.

「可是路途這麼遙遠，」安娜嘆了口氣說，「我怎麼可能到得了那裡？」

「我可以用摩托車載妳去呀！」奶奶回答說。

「哇塞！」安娜大叫。一轉眼，她就已經坐上奶奶那輛超級摩托車，戴著幾乎要遮到眼睛的安全帽，一路狂飆而行。

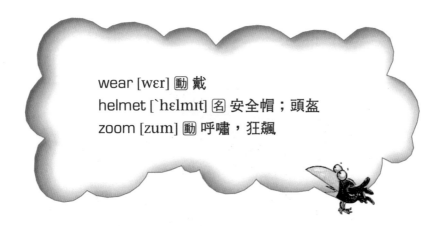

wear [wɛr] 勔 戴
helmet [`hɛlmɪt] 名 安全帽；頭盔
zoom [zum] 勔 呼嘯，狂飆

Anna had written her mum and dad a quick note to **explain** where she was going, so they wouldn't worry about her.

The motorbike **gobbled** up the miles and they soon left the town behind. Granny sang sea-**shanties** and **pirate** songs as they whooshed along. At this speed they would get to Uncle Oscar's island in no time!

Crunch! Grinch! Grunch! Gronch! Ptoing! Put-put-bleeergh! Splooooooooop!

"Oh dear," said Granny as the motorbike came to a **grinding halt** at the roadside. "Something is very wrong. Oh, pooh! Now what shall we do?"

安娜留了一張便條給爸爸媽媽，向他們解釋她的去處，請他們不要擔心。

摩托車飛奔了好幾英里，一下子就離城鎮老遠，奶奶沿途高唱著船歌和海盜歌。照這種速度，他們很快就可以到達奧斯卡叔叔的島嶼了。

砰！啪！鏗鏘！──噗──噗──噗！

「老天！」奶奶叫了一聲，摩托車噼噼呼呼地在路旁停住了。「看來情況不妙。唉！現在該怎麼辦呢？」

explain [ɪk`splen] 動 解釋
gobble [`gɑbl] 動 狼吞虎嚥《up》
shanty = chanty [`ʃæntɪ] 名 船歌
pirate [`paɪrət] 名 海盜
grinding [`graɪndɪŋ] 形 嘎嘎響的
halt [hɔlt] 名 停止

They both climbed off the motorbike. Anna sat on a grassy **slope** while Granny **muttered** at the motorbike and hit it here and there with a large **spanner**.

"Do you know what's wrong?" asked Anna.

"Yes," said Granny. "The twinge-flange is broken. It's a very simple **repair**. All it needs is a new twinge-flange." Granny sighed. "I haven't got a new twinge-flange."

第三章

　　她們倆爬下摩托車。安娜坐在斜坡的草地上，奶奶對著摩托車喃喃自語，手上拿著一支大扳手到處敲敲打打。

　　「妳知道是哪裡出問題嗎？」安娜問。

　　「當然啦！」奶奶說，「齒輪壞掉了，這很容易修理，只要換個新的齒輪就好了。」奶奶嘆口氣說，「可惜我現在沒有新的齒輪。」

slope [slop] 名 斜坡
mutter [ˋmʌtɚ] 動 嘀咕 《at》
spanner [ˋspænɚ] 名 扳手
　（美式用法為 wrench [rɛntʃ]）
repair [rɪˋpɛr] 名 修理

"**O**h, dear," said Anna. Then she said. "Hello, what's this?" as a dark, round shadow came **creeping** across the grass.

They both looked up. It was a huge red **hot-air balloon**.

"Hello down there," called a woman wearing a flying-helmet and **goggles**. "Lovely day for it." And she waved cheerfully.

"Excuse me," Anna called, "do you have a **spare** twinge-flange you could lend us?"

「喔！老天！」安娜應著。「嘿，這是什麼？」有個黑黑圓圓的東西漸漸經過草地上方。

　　她們倆抬頭一看，竟然是一個巨大的紅色熱氣球。

　　「下面的人啊，你們好。」一個頭頂飛行帽、眼戴護目鏡的女人大聲叫著。她興高采烈地揮手說：「真是適合飛行的好天氣。」

　　「對不起，」安娜大叫，「您有備用齒輪可以借給我們嗎？」

creep [krip] 動 漸漸出現
hot-air balloon 熱氣球
goggles [`gɑglz] 名 護目鏡
spare [spɛr] 形 備用的

"I'm afraid not," said the **balloonist**. "But you're very welcome to come **aboard**. I'll take you to the nearest town. I'm sure someone there will have what you need."

A rope ladder came **spinning** down from the balloon's wicker basket. Anna and her granny climbed up and the balloonist rolled the ladder back up again.

The balloonist pulled a **lever** and a **propeller** began to turn. Anna **leaned** over the edge of the basket. Her granny's motorbike already looked like a toy. Soon it was just a tiny dot as the balloon **chugged** along over open countryside.

「恐怕沒有吧！」熱氣球飛行員回答說。「不過歡迎妳們上來，我可以載妳們到最近的城鎮，我想那裡一定有人有妳們要的東西。」

一條繩梯從熱氣球的藤籃中慢慢降下來，安娜和奶奶登上熱氣球後，飛行員把繩梯捲起來收好。

飛行員將一個桿子往後拉，螺旋推進器便馬上轉動起來。安娜靠在籃邊往下看，奶奶的摩托車已經變得像個玩具一樣大了。熱氣球轟轟作響，飛越廣闊的鄉間，不一會兒，摩托車看起來只剩下一個小黑點。

balloonist [bə`lunɪst] 图 乘熱氣球的人
aboard [ə`bɔrd] 副 上飛機，上船
spin [spɪn] 動 旋轉
lever [`lɛvɚ] 图 桿
propeller [prə`pɛlɚ] 图 螺旋槳，推進器
lean [lin] 動 倚靠
chug [tʃʌg] 動 轟轟作響

"Care for a sandwich?" asked the balloonist opening a large wicker **hamper**. Anna and her granny and the balloonist all sat down to eat.

Suddenly there was a terrible **roaring** noise. Rooaaarrrrrr. Whoooooooosh.

Something long and thin and silver-colored **burst** right through the balloon with a huge *BANG!*

「想來份三明治嗎？」飛行員邊打開大籃子邊問著。於是安娜、奶奶和飛行員都坐下來吃東西。

忽然，傳來一陣恐怖的巨響。

轟！轟！轟！咻——砰！

有個細細長長、銀灰色的東西，突然砰地一聲巨響，不偏不倚地衝破了熱氣球。

hamper [ˋhæmpɚ] 名（有蓋的）大籃子
roaring [ˋrorɪŋ] 形 轟隆作響的
burst [bɝst] 動 突然出現

Anna and her granny **clung** on for dear life as the basket **rocked** and the balloon **sagged** and **hissed**.

The balloonist looked over the side. "**Bangers** and **mash**!" she said. "We're going to **crash**!"

But they didn't crash. They came down very softly, as though they had landed in a giant heap of feathers.

籃子搖搖晃晃，熱氣球嘶、嘶、嘶地直往下墜，安娜和奶奶死命地緊緊抱著。

　　「不會吧！」飛行員向旁邊看了一眼說，「我們要墜毀了。」

　　然而她們並沒有墜毀，她們輕輕柔柔地落下，好像降落在一大堆羽毛上。

cling [klɪŋ] 動 緊抓
（過去式clung [klʌŋ]）
rock [rɑk] 動 搖晃
sag [sæg] 動 下降
hiss [hɪs] 動 發出嘶聲
crash [kræʃ] 動 墜落

Chapter Four

A few seconds later an **anxious** face **peered** over the side of the basket.

"I'm terribly sorry," said the **bald-headed** man, looking worriedly at the three people in the basket. "You got in the way of an **experiment** of mine."

He helped them out of the basket. Nearby was a small **concrete bunker** with a long metal tube sticking out of the roof.

Anna climbed out of the basket and fell waist-deep into feathers.

第四章

幾秒鐘後，一張緊張兮兮的臉從籃子外邊往裡頭瞄。

「我真的很抱歉，」一位禿頭先生滿臉愁容地望著籃中的三個人說，「妳們闖入我的實驗區了。」

接著，他協助她們爬出籃子。附近有一個小小的混凝土壕溝，頂部伸出一條長長的金屬管子。

安娜爬出籃子，一頭栽進深及腰部的羽毛堆中。

anxious [`æŋ(k)ʃəs] 形 憂慮的
peer [pɪr] 動 盯著看
bald-headed [`bɔld`hɛdɪd] 形 禿頭的
experiment [ɪk`spɛrəmənt] 名 動 實驗
concrete [`kankrit] 形 混凝土的
bunker [`bʌŋkɚ] 名 壕溝

"**I**'m experimenting with **rockets**," said the man, helping Anna to her feet. "These feathers are to **save** the rockets from getting bent when they crash." He sighed. "They nearly all crash," he said. "You see, the problem is that they really need **pilots**." He pointed to himself. "I can't pilot them because I have to press the button that fires them." He **blinked** at Anna and her granny."

I don't **suppose** either of you know how to pilot a rocket?" he asked hopefully.

「我在實驗火箭啦！」這位先生一邊扶起安娜，一邊說。「這些羽毛可以防止火箭墜落時彎曲變形。」他又嘆了口氣說。「差一點就全毀了，妳們瞧，問題就是沒有人可以駕駛這些火箭。」他指著自己說。「可是我不能親自駕駛，因為我必須按發射鈕呀！」他對著安娜和奶奶眨了眨眼。

　　「妳們有人會駕駛火箭嗎？」他滿懷希望地問。

rocket [ˋrɑkɪt] 名 火箭
save [sev] 動 防止
pilot [ˋpaɪlət] 名 駕駛員 動 駕駛
blink [blɪŋk] 動 眨眼《at》
suppose [səˋpoz] 動 猜想

"**I**'m a quick learner," said Anna helpfully.

"I'm off," said the balloonist. "I can't stand rockets!"

The bald-headed man led Anna and her granny to his bunker. "It's really very simple," he said as he **strapped** Anna into a seat in the **nose-cone** of the rocket. He showed her the **controls** while her granny **squeezed** into the **co-pilot**'s seat.

The man closed the nose-cone door. Over the **intercom** Anna heard:

"Fivefourthreetwoone! **Blast off!**"

「我學東西很快。」安娜熱心地回答。

「我要走了，」熱氣球飛行員說，「我最受不了火箭了。」

禿頭先生帶著安娜和奶奶來到壕溝。「這真的很簡單。」他邊說邊用安全帶把安娜繫在火箭艙的座位上。他還向安娜說明了火箭的操控裝置；奶奶則努力擠進副駕駛的座位裡。

這位先生關起火箭艙門，透過對講機，安娜聽到：

「五、四、三、二、一，發射！」

strap [stræp] 勔（用帶子）綁
nost-cone [`noz‚kon] 名（火箭的）頭部
control [kən`trol] 名 控制裝置
（常用 controls）
squeeze [skwiz] 勔 擠入
co-pilot [ko`paɪlət] 名 副駕駛
intercom [`ɪntɚ‚kɑm] 名 對講機
blast off 發射，升空

Anna was pressed back in her seat as the rocket shot into the air.

They burst through a cloud and came out into brilliant sunshine. Anna waved at a very surprised-looking bird. For a while all they could see was the blue sky. Then the blueness got darker. Then it got darker still. And **all of a sudden** it was quite black and the whole sky was full of stars.

"It's night-time!" said Anna.

"No, it's not," said her granny. "We're in **outer space**!"

火箭朝天空飛衝出去，安娜整個人往後貼在椅子上。

　　他們衝過白雲，飛進耀眼奪目的陽光裡，安娜還向一臉吃驚的小鳥揮一揮手呢！有好一段時間，他們只看見藍藍的天空，然後顏色由藍轉暗，越來越暗。突然間，四周都變黑了，整個天空都佈滿了星星。

　　「晚上了。」安娜說。

　　「不，不是晚上，」奶奶回答說，「是我們到外太空了。」

all of a sudden　突然
outer space　外太空

A roly-poly satellite cartwheeled by, making a beeping noise. The rocket shot twice around the satellite and then headed downwards.

"Wheeeee!" shouted Anna as the sky turned blue again. A few moments later she could see the whole of the country spread out like a weather map, green and friendly in the blue of the sea.

The land got bigger and bigger, and the rocket went faster and faster. Suddenly all Anna could see was mountains rushing up toward the rocket.

一個圓滾滾的人造衛星經過他們，發出嗶嗶嗶的嘈雜聲，火箭繞著它轉了兩圈，就朝下方飛去。

「耶！」安娜一看到天空又變回藍色，高興得歡呼了起來。一會兒，她便看見整片翠綠、祥和的鄉野，像張天氣圖般，伸展在藍藍的海上。

地面變得越來越大，火箭的速度也越來越快。突然間，安娜只見群山直逼火箭而來。

roly-poly [`rolɪ,polɪ] 形 圓滾滾的，胖嘟嘟的
satellite [`sætl̩,aɪt] 名 人造衛星
cartwheel [`kɑrt,hwil] 動 側翻
beep [bip] 動 嗶嗶地響

"**O**h! Help!" said Anna as an especially tall peak came **galloping** toward them.

There was a gentle **bump**, a **slide** and a **slither** and a *whumph*! as the rocket came to a halt on the highest slopes of the snowy mountainside.

「哦！救命哪！」安娜看見一座奇陡無比的山峰直撲過來，尖聲大叫了起來。

然後輕輕一撞，火箭便慢慢往下滑——滑——砰！火箭停在山腹積雪的陡坡上。

gallop [`ɡæləp] 勔 高速接近
bump [bʌmp] 名 碰撞
slide [slaɪd] 名 滑行
slither [`slɪðɚ] 名 滑行

Chapter Five

A red light **winked on and off** in front of Anna.

"*Open in case of* **emergency**," Anna read. She opened the drawer and pulled out two pairs of **rollerblades**.

"How very useful," said her granny as the two of them climbed out of the rocket. The snow was only a little cap on the top of the mountain. They walked down to where the snow ended and put on their rollerblades.

第五章

有個紅燈在安娜面前閃啊閃的。

安娜看到上面寫著：「緊急情況時請打開此處！」她打開抽屜，拉出兩雙溜冰鞋。

「還真有用！」他們爬出火箭時，奶奶說。還好，雪只堆積在山頂上。一走到雪地盡頭，他們便穿上溜冰鞋。

wink [wɪŋk] 動 閃動
on and off 斷斷續續
emergency [ɪˋmɝdʒənsɪ] 名 緊急情況
rollerblade [ˋrolɚ͵bled] 名 溜冰鞋

"**N**ow then," said Anna. "We will probably go very fast, so we should hold hands."

Anna took a **tight** hold of her granny's hand.

"One, two, three, GO!"

Vwoooooooooooooom!

Hand in hand they shot down the mountainside like **pellets** from a **catapult**. Every now and then Anna had to **adjust** her **balance** so she didn't fall over. She found out that she was very good at rollerblading.

「這樣一來，」安娜說，「我們可能會衝得很快，所以最好還是手牽著手吧！」

安娜緊緊握著奶奶的手。

「一、二、三，衝呀！」

咻……

她們像從彈弓發射出的彈丸，手牽手從山腹俯衝而下。安娜不時得調整身體的平衡以免跌倒；她發現自己真是個溜冰高手呢！

tight [taɪt] 形 緊緊的

pellet [ˋpɛlɪt] 名 彈丸

catapult [ˋkætəˌpʌlt] 名 彈弓
動 把…有力地射出

adjust [əˋdʒʌst] 動 調整

balance [ˋbæləns] 名 平衡

They came to a deep **valley** and before they knew it they had crossed the bottom and were **whipping** up the other side and over a sharp edge. For a few seconds they hung in mid air before they landed again and whooshed down the next slope.

Anna got used to it. Whoosh down into a valley. Wheee! up the next slope! Yeehaaah! as they flew into the air and Thumpetty! as they landed on the next bit of mountain.

Wheee!

她們一路滑向深谷，不知不覺中便已飛過谷底、衝向對面，甚至躍過陡峭的懸崖。她們騰空了幾秒，落地後馬上咻地一聲又衝下另一個山坡。

　　安娜已經習慣了，咻地一聲衝下山谷，呼地一聲又登上斜坡。耶！她們飛上了天空，然後又咚地一聲，降落在另一座山上。

　　哇……

valley [ˋvælɪ] 名 山谷
whip [hwɪp] 動 快速移動

Yee-haaah!

"Oops!" said Anna.

SPLASHAROONIE!

The mountains had ended. Anna and her granny had flown over the last **ridge** and splooshed straight into water.

Anna **spluttered**. It was salt water. They were in the sea. Anna was just trying to remember how to swim when something long and rounded and **sleek** came up under her and she found herself sitting **astride** a **dolphin**.

耶——啊！

「哦哦！」安娜叫了一聲。

噗通一聲！

沒有山了。安娜和奶奶越過最後一個山脈，噗通一聲一頭栽進水裡。

安娜語無倫次地唸了一堆。水鹹鹹的，原來她們掉到海裡了。安娜正努力回想該怎麼游泳，就突然有個長長圓圓、全身光溜溜的東西靠到她身子底下。等她回過神來，已經跨坐在一隻海豚的背上了。

ridge [rɪdʒ] 名 山脊，山脈
splutter [`splʌtə] 動 急切地說
sleek [slik] 形 光滑的
astride [ə`straɪd] 介 跨騎在…上
dolphin [`dɑlfɪn] 名 海豚

She **wiped** the water out of her eyes and saw that her granny was sitting on an even bigger dolphin.

"That was a bit of luck!" said Granny with a **grin**.

Before Anna could think of a reply, the two dolphins began swimming at a great speed out into the open sea.

""Hey!" said Anna, **tapping** gently on her dolphin's head. She pointed back to the land. "We want to go that way!"

"Chik! Chik! Chik! Chi-h-ih-ih-ik,"said the dolphin.

她把眼睛周圍的水抹掉，看見奶奶坐在一隻更大的海豚上面。

「還真是幸運呢！」奶奶咧嘴笑著說。

安娜還來不及回答，兩隻海豚已經急速向大海挺進。

「嘿！」安娜叫著，手輕輕地拍著海豚的頭。「我們要去那裡！」她轉身指著陸地說。

「咿！咿！咿！咿——」海豚回答說。

wipe [waɪp] 勔 擦拭
grin [grɪn] 图 咧嘴微笑
tap [tæp] 勔 拍打

"Granny," Anna called.  "Do you speak dolphin?"

"I'm afraid not," said her granny. "I think we'll just have to trust them to take us somewhere safe."

It wasn't long before the land dropped below the **horizon** and they were out in the empty sea.

Where **on earth** were the dolphins going?

Suddenly Anna noticed a **shoal** of flying fish all **dipping** in and out of the water together. As the shoal came closer Anna could hear tiny **high-pitched** voices all singing **in chorus**.

「奶奶，」安娜大喊，「您會不會說海豚話？」

「不會耶！」奶奶說，「看來我們只好相信牠們會載我們到安全的地方囉！」

沒過多久，陸地從地平線上消失，她們游向一望無垠的海洋。

這些海豚究竟要游到哪裡呢？

突然間，安娜發現一大群飛魚在海面跳上跳下，牠們越游越近。安娜聽見細細尖尖的魚聲好像在唱和著。

horizon [hə`raɪzn̩] 图 地平線
on earth 究竟
shoal [ʃol] 图 群
dip [dɪp] 動 浸
high-pitched [`haɪ`pɪtʃt] 形 高而尖銳的
in chorus 合唱地，齊聲地

She stared in **amazement** as the cloud of leaping fish got closer and closer until she could hear exactly what they were singing.

"Happy birthday to you, happy birthday to you, happy birthday dear Anna, happy birthday to you!" they sang. And then there was a burst of cheering and laughter as the shoal of fish dived one last time back into the water and **disappeared**.

她驚訝地盯著這群跳來跳去的魚兒，看牠們愈來愈近，這才聽清楚牠們唱的是：

　　「祝妳生日快樂，祝妳生日快樂，祝妳生日快樂，祝安娜生日快樂！」一陣歡呼聲後，這群魚兒潛入水中，消失得無影無蹤。

amazement [ə`mezmənt] 名 驚訝
disappear [,dɪsə`pɪr] 動 消失

Chapter Six

"This is very **odd**," thought Anna. "How did they know it was my birthday?"

"Land ho!" called Anna's granny. Anna looked over to where she was pointing. It was funny-looking land, she thought. It was perfectly flat and very small.

As they got closer, Anna could see that it was a wooden **raft**. On the raft sat a woman in a **deck chair** reading a newspaper.

"Hello Polly!" said the woman, jumping up. "Hello Dolly!"

第六章

「這真的很奇怪，」安娜想，「牠們怎麼知道今天是我的生日呢？」

「是陸地——耶！」奶奶喊著。安娜順著奶奶指的方向望過去。這陸地長得可真奇怪啊！她心想。又小又平的。

等她們靠近點，安娜發現那只是塊木筏；木筏上有一個女人坐在帆布椅上看報紙。

「哈囉，寶莉！」女人站起身來說，「哈囉，朵莉!」

odd [ɑd] 形 古怪的
raft [ræft] 名 筏
deck chair（折疊）帆布躺椅

"Er, my name's Anna," said Anna. "Not Polly or Dolly. And this is my granny."

The woman grinned the toothiest grin that Anna had ever seen. "I was saying hello to my two dolphin friends here," she said as she helped Anna and her granny on to the raft. "Are you lost? We don't get many visitors up here."

"We're looking for the Isle of Chyppes," said Anna.

「嗯……我叫安娜，」安娜回答說，「不是寶莉也不是朵莉。這位是我奶奶。」

這女人笑得露出了整排牙齒，安娜可沒見過這麼道地的笑容哩！「我在向那兩隻海豚朋友打招呼。」她邊說邊幫忙安娜和奶奶爬上木筏。「迷路了嗎？我們這兒不常有訪客哦！」

「我們要去凱普斯島。」安娜說。

"**W**ell, well," said the raft woman. "I think I can help you." She led Anna and her granny to the far side of the raft, where a tiny motor boat was **moored**, **bobbing** in the **choppy** water.

"I'm afraid there isn't room for both of you on board," said the raft woman. "Would one of you mind **water-skiing** along behind?"

Anna **volunteered** to water-ski. Her granny and the raft woman climbed into the tiny boat and the **motor** started.

「這個嘛……」木筏上的女人說，「或許我可以幫上忙。」她帶安娜和奶奶到木筏遠遠的另一頭，那裡泊著一艘小汽艇，正隨著波浪起起伏伏。

　　「恐怕船坐不下妳們倆喲！」木筏上的女人說。「妳們其中一人可不可以跟在後頭滑水前進呢？」

　　安娜自願滑水；奶奶和木筏上的女人則爬上小汽艇發動引擎。

moor [mur] 動 繫住
bob [bab] 動 上下浮動
choppy [`tʃɑpɪ] 形 波濤洶湧的
water-ski [`wɔtɚ͵ski] 動 滑水
volunteer [͵vɑlən`tɪr] 動 志願
motor [`motɚ] 名 引擎

"**H**old on tight," said the raft woman, "And remember — keep your knees slightly bent and try to *ride* the bigger waves."

The boat shot off. Anna took a **firm grip** of the rope.

"I hope I can **manage** this," she said to herself. "I hope I don't — whoooooooooooooooo-oooooooooop!"

For a few moments Anna couldn't tell whether she was on her feet or her **elbow** or her left ear. Water flooded past her in great white **sprays** and it felt like her arms were being pulled off.

「抓穩了，」木筏上的女人喊著，「記住膝蓋要微彎，而且要儘量『乘』大浪前進哦！」

小艇飛奔了起來；安娜緊緊地抓著繩子。

「希望我還應付得了，」安娜自言自語地說，「我不希望會……哦——」

有好一段時間安娜完全弄不清楚她是用腳在滑水，還是用手肘，還是用左耳。海浪激起的白色的水花向她直衝過來，安娜覺得手臂好像快被扯斷了。

firm [fɝm] 形 穩穩的
grip [grɪp] 名 緊握
manage [`mænɪdʒ] 動 控制
elbow [`ɛl,bo] 名 肘
spray [spre] 名 水花

But then she got her balance and started to enjoy herself. She even tried a few tricks while her granny watched from the back of the boat. Holding on with one hand. Lifting one leg in the air. Lifting the other leg in the air.

She was having a thoroughly good time when the little boat took a sudden turn to the left and Anna lost her grip on the **towrope**.

With a yell, Anna found herself speeding toward a small **hump** of land with a tall tower in its very middle. Anna **waggled** her arms and **wobbled** her legs as she tried to keep upright on the water-skis.

可是，她很快就恢復平衡，而且開始自得其樂。奶奶從小艇後頭望過來，她還表演了幾個特技：單手握繩、兩腳交換懸空前進。

她正滑得開心極了，突然，小船向左急轉彎，安娜鬆掉了手中的繩子。

她尖叫了一聲，整個人衝向一塊凸起的、正中央矗立著一座高塔的小陸地。安娜甩甩手，抖抖腳，想在划水板上挺直身體。

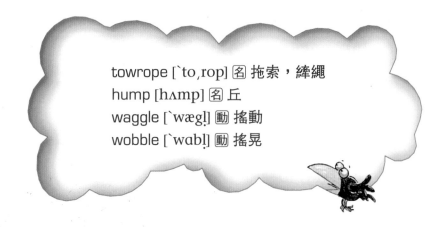

towrope [`to,rop] 图 拖索，縴繩
hump [hʌmp] 图 丘
waggle [`wægl̩] 動 搖動
wobble [`wɑbl̩] 動 搖晃

She zoomed up the sandy beach. The skis came to a **shuddering** halt and Anna was catapulted head over heels into a thick **bush**.

She **clambered** out, **plucking** bits of twig and leaf out of her hair. She looked back to see where the boat had got to. But of the boat there was not the slightest sign.

Anna walked up the path that led to the lonely tower.

On the huge black wooden door hung a **crooked** sign.

她朝著沙灘跑了過去。滑水板抖了一下驟然停住，使得安娜栽了一個大筋斗，掉進茂密的樹叢中。

　　她費了番功夫爬出來，扯掉黏在頭髮上的小樹枝、樹葉，再回頭找找小汽艇的蹤影，可是什麼也沒看見。

　　安娜沿著小路走向那座孤單的碉堡！

　　黑色的木頭大門上掛著一個歪曲的牌子。

shudder [`ʃʌdə] 動 顫抖
bush [buʃ] 名 灌木叢
clamber [`klæmbə] 動 手腳並用地爬
pluck [plʌk] 動 拔掉
crooked [`krukɪd] 形 歪斜的，彎曲的

Oscar's Tower, it said. "Aha!" said Anna to herself. "I've landed on the Isle of Chyppes! Brilliant!"

No **hawkers**, said the crooked sign. No **circulars**, no sellers of **double-glazing** or **central heating**. No visitors of any sort whatsoever. This means YOU!

"It can't really mean me," Anna thought as she pressed the doorbell under a sign which said: DON'T RING!

上面寫著：奧斯卡碉堡。

「啊哈！」安娜對自己大叫，「我居然到了凱普斯島，太帥了！」

歪歪的牌子上寫著：嚴禁小販、廣告傳單、雙層玻璃或空調推銷員；嚴禁各式各樣的訪客，意思就是——你！

「這不會真的指我吧！」安娜想著，順手按下門鈴，結果看見門鈴上的牌子寫著：「禁止按鈴」。

hawker [`hɔkɚ] 名 小販
circular [`sɝkjələ] 名 廣告傳單
double-glazing [ˌdʌbl̩`glezɪŋ] 名 雙層玻璃
central heating 中央暖氣系統

Chapter Seven

Anna waited. There was the sound of **hollow**, echoey footsteps. Anna waited a bit longer. **Eventually** the huge door **creaked** slowly open and an **impressive** moustache appeared somewhere near the top.

"Hello, Uncle Oscar!" exclaimed Anna. "I'm your niece, Anna, and it's my birthday today in case you forgot!"

A pair of twinkly eyes peered down at Anna from above a long **lumpy** nose.

第七章

　　安娜等候著，聽見腳步聲空洞的回音；安娜又等了一會兒。大門終於慢慢地、嘰嘰嘎嘎地打開來了，一個造型特殊的大鬍子出現在門頂附近。

　　「嗨！奧斯卡叔叔，」安娜興奮地大叫，「我是您的姪女安娜，順便提醒您今天是我的生日。」

　　一雙閃閃發亮的眼睛從滿是疙瘩的大鼻子上往下看著安娜。

hollow [`halo] 形 空洞的
eventually [ɪ`vɛntʃʊəlɪ] 副 結果，終於
creak [krik] 動 發出嘎嘎聲
impressive [ɪm`prɛsɪv] 形 令人印象深刻的
lumpy [`lʌmpɪ] 形 滿是疙瘩的

"**I**'ve been expecting you," said Uncle Oscar with a huge **beaming** smile. "Come on in, my dear, and a happy birthday to you!"

"Excuse me," said Anna as she stepped over the **threshold** into a long dark **corridor**. "But you *can't* have been expecting me."

"Oh, but I was," said Uncle Oscar as he led Anna toward a big pair of closed doors. "We *all* were!"

「我一直在等妳，」奧斯卡露出最愉快的笑容說，「快進來，我的寶貝，祝妳生日快樂！」

　　「對不起，」安娜跨過門檻，走進暗暗的長廊說著，「您怎麼可能在等我呢？」

　　「我是在等妳呀！」奧斯卡叔叔邊說邊領著安娜來到另一扇大門前面。「我們都在等呀！」

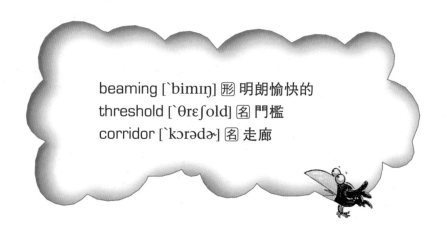

beaming [`bimɪŋ] 形 明朗愉快的
threshold [`θrɛʃold] 名 門檻
corridor [`kɔrədɚ] 名 走廊

Uncle Oscar opened the doors. Anna was almost **bowled over** by a huge cheer! The room beyond was **decorated** for a party. There was a table filled with food and drinks and the room was filled with people.

Anna stood there with her mouth hanging open. Mum and Dad were there. So was Granny. So was the balloonist and the man with the rockets. And so was the raft woman. As well as all Anna's friends from school and all her other uncles and aunts and cousins.

Uncle Oscar pushed Anna into the party room and everyone started singing "Happy Birthday to You"!

Mum and Dad gave her a big **hug**. "Surprise!"

"But... but..." said Anna. "But I thought Uncle Oscar had forgotten!"

"Not a bit of it," said Uncle Oscar. He pulled a piece of paper out of his pocket. "Now then," he said. "Let's see if I remembered everything."

奧斯卡叔叔打開門，安娜差一點就被滿屋子熱烈的歡呼聲給嚇到。整個房間佈置得像派對一樣，桌上堆滿了食物和飲料，還有好多好多人。

安娜整個人呆住了，嘴巴張得好大。爸爸媽媽在裡面、奶奶在裡面、熱氣球飛行員和發射火箭的先生在裡面、木筏上的女人在裡面，連學校的朋友、叔叔阿姨、堂兄弟姊妹們也都在裡面。

bowl over 使驚嚇
decorate [ˋdɛkəˌret] 動 裝飾

奧斯卡叔叔把安娜推進慶生會的房間內，然後大家開始高聲唱著：「生日快樂」！

　　爸爸媽媽緊緊抱著安娜說：「嚇一跳吧！」

　　「嗯……可是……」安娜說，「可是人家以為奧斯卡叔叔早就忘記了！」

　　「才沒咧！」奧斯卡叔叔說，然後從口袋拿出一張單子。「現在來看看我是不是每一件事都沒忘啊！」

hug [hʌg] 名 擁抱

79

Anna **recognized** the sheet of paper. It was the list of birthday presents she had sent to Uncle Oscar.

Uncle Oscar began to read the list.

"I would like a ride on a motorbike, please!" he read. "Or I would like to have a go in a hot-air balloon. Or I would like to see how a rocket works." Uncle Oscar **ticked** each **request off** with a red pen. "Yes, yes, yes," he said.

安娜認出了那張單子，那是她寄給奧斯卡叔叔的生日禮物清單。

　　奧斯卡叔叔開始唸著單子。

　　「我想騎摩托車，拜託！或者搭乘熱氣球，不然就讓我親眼目睹火箭升空。」奧斯卡叔叔每唸完一項就用紅筆打勾，然後說：「完成，完成，完成。」

recognize [`rɛkəg,naɪz] 勔 認出
tick [tɪk] 勔 在…上標記號，打勾
tick off 在…上標記號，打勾
request [rɪ`kwɛst] 名 要求

Then he carried on reading. "I would like a pair of rollerblades," he read. "I would like to meet a dolphin. I would also like to learn to water-ski. And most of all, I would like a big party."

Uncle Oscar ticked away with his red pen. "Yes, yes, yes," he said. "And finally: YES!"

And everyone laughed and cheered as Anna was led to the seat of **honor** at the end of the table.

然後他繼續唸著。「我想要一雙溜冰鞋、我想看看海豚、學滑水，最重要的是我想要有一個熱鬧的慶生會。」

　　奧斯卡叔叔用紅筆一項項地打勾，同時唸著：「完成，完成，完成。」最後說：「都完成了。」

　　安娜被帶到餐桌一端的貴賓席，大家都興高采烈地歡呼。

honor [`ɑnɚ] 名 榮譽

"And I thought you'd forgotten!" she said with the biggest smile she had ever smiled.

It was the best birthday present Anna had ever been given. And to top it all, everyone was taken home afterwards by **submarine**. As Anna told her mum as she **snuggled** happily into bed that night, a ride in a submarine was something she had *thought* of putting on the birthday present list, but she had left it off because she didn't want Uncle Oscar to think she was being **greedy**.

「我以為您早就忘得一乾二淨了！」安娜說著，露出了最最燦爛的笑容。

　　這的確是安娜有史以來最棒的生日禮物！還有，後來大家都是搭潛水艇回家的。那晚，安娜開心地躺在床上告訴媽媽說，她本來想把「搭乘潛水艇」列在生日禮物清單上，不過後來放棄了，因為她不想讓奧斯卡叔叔認為她是個貪心的女孩！

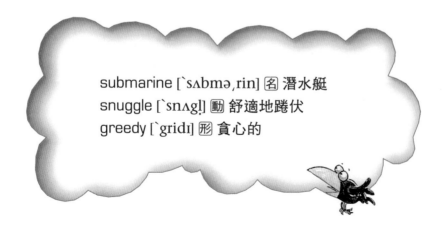

submarine [`sʌbməˌrin] 图 潛水艇
snuggle [`snʌgl̩] 動 舒適地踡伏
greedy [`gridɪ] 形 貪心的

中英對照，既可學英語又可了解偉人小故事哦！

超級科學家系列
SUPER SCIENTISTS

當彗星掠過哈雷眼前，
當蘋果落在牛頓頭頂，
當電燈泡在愛迪生手中亮起……
一個個求知的心靈與真理所碰撞出的火花，
就是《超級科學家系列》！

神祕元素：居禮夫人的故事
電燈的發明：愛迪生的故事
望遠天際：伽利略的故事
光的顏色：牛頓的故事
爆炸性的發現：諾貝爾的故事
蠶寶寶的祕密：巴斯德的故事Ⅱ
宇宙教授：愛因斯坦的故事
命運的彗星：哈雷的故事

英語發音

黃正興編著

想要說一口又溜又標準的
英語嗎？
想要知道怎麼樣把英文歌
唱得更正確好聽嗎？

國家圖書館出版品預行編目資料

安娜生日探險記 = Anna's birthday adventure
/ Allan Frewin Jones 著；Judy Brown 繪；
三民書局編輯部譯――初版. ――臺北市：
三民，民88
面；　公分
ISBN 957–14–3003–X（平裝）

1.英國語言―讀本

805.18　　　　　　　　　88004009

網際網路位址　http : // www. sanmin. com. tw

ⓒ 安娜生日探險記

著作人　Allan Frewin Jones
繪圖者　Judy Brown
譯　者　三民書局編輯部
發行人　劉振強
著作財　三民書局股份有限公司
產權人
　　　　臺北市復興北路三八六號
發行所　三民書局股份有限公司
　　　　地址 / 臺北市復興北路三八六號
　　　　電話 / 二五〇〇六六〇〇
　　　　郵撥 / 〇〇〇九九九八――五號
印刷所　三民書局股份有限公司
門市部　復北店 / 臺北市復興北路三八六號
　　　　重南店 / 臺北市重慶南路一段六十一號
初　版　中華民國八十八年九月
編　號　S85480
定　價　新臺幣壹佰陸拾元整
行政院新聞局登記證局版臺業字第〇二〇〇號

有著作權　不准侵害

ISBN　957–14–3003–X（平裝）